The Love Wave

The Love Wave

DINA HUSSEINI

To order additional copies of this book, contact:
Xlibris Corporation
0-800-644-6988
www.xlibrispublishing.co.uk
Orders@xlibrispublishing.co.uk
302276

Dedication Page

Great, Grand, Mother, YiaYia Theodosia (R.I.P): *"You said I would do something that would change how people view me; now I have! Thank you for looking over me every single day! I love you and I miss you!"*

Papu Fivos (R.I.P): *"You have gone but your spirit is still with us. We will miss you always. Thank you for talking to me even though it was for a little while."*

Lakis (My Dearest and Bravest Uncle): *"Your strength and power for survival has driven me to do many things now that I am young and able. I have gained a great amount of individuality through your drive for being here."*

Maria (My one-of-a-kind-Mother): *"People envy us and it is immense because I know that you are my reason for eternal greatness. I know that days go by we do not speak knowing that our thoughts connect non-the-less. I am glad you are my mother and I cherish every moment of joy, tears, anger, hate and love; because a mother like you, mum, there is no other."*

Ahmad (My # 1 Father): *"Your patients and support throughout everything I do and want to do is in abundance! Dad, one word can describe you and I say it with an open – heart, GENEROUS! Thank you for never giving up!"*

Ramzi (My Angel Brother): *"Your presence and understanding means more to me than anything else. It is hard without you beside me but I need to find my way and you, yours. I have found my calling. What is yours?"*

Nasa (My Awesome Aunt): *"Great things happen to those who wait and I waited and now, I will be waiting for more great things to come. Thank you for never doubting me even when words were thrown at you that you did not deserve."*

Family in Cyprus, UK, UAE, and Lebanon (You know who you are): *"It is great to dream, but dream something you can get, because you will get it. Dreams are cars that can get you to your destination without tough roads. The best feeling in life is your accomplishments. Go and get them!!!"*

YiaYia Georgia (My Grandmother From a Distance): *"Se Ibere Efkharisto. S'aghabo Yiayiakamu poli!!"*

Peter (My Best Friend): *"No one can or will ever take your place. You are a friend in a million and I am very happy that we have become so close. Thank you for always being around!"*

I was coming out of the bathroom when I saw Jason, drunk as usual, standing outside; waiting for me. He looked into in my eyes and said, "I have missed you so much." I looked at him and smiled; then I said, "I moved on Jason; so should you." For a moment we were just standing there looking at each other. He was shaking; and yet I did not care as I used to.

He approached me suddenly and everything changed between us; I thought he was going to hug me but instead he pushed me against the wall and began kissing me. I tried to push him off but he was too strong. I screamed and kicked him between his legs.

I thought no one heard me because of the loud music but, to my surprise, Tom came to my rescue; "What is going on here?" Tom asked in disappointment. Jason got up looked at both of us and then walked away. Tom approached me and I screamed; then I ran off leaving Tom on his own to think about what just happened?

To end what just happened, let me tell you how it all began. In the summer of July 2002, I graduated from High School. I was glad I got rid of that school because I was not happy and my grades were horrible. I was bullied constantly. I extremely hated my school that I thought of killing every single person in it. Luckily, it was just a mere thought in my mind and nothing serious happened.

Yes, I was bullied every day; I was bullied by teachers and students. I had no friends and I did not make the effort to make any friends, either. My parents were happy that I graduated because they never thought I could. To their surprise, I shocked them. I was happy I was out and now I could go and *write*!

I applied to many colleges to have an academic degree while I was pursuing my dream. I was planning on going for a degree in Philosophy/Theology where I could explore new things as well as write. Knowledge is important these days for you to be aware of your surroundings. My family members advised me to go in that path of studies. This type of major can enrich me in both knowledge and writing skills; not to mention that while I was studying, I would also be writing.

One day, in September 2002, I sat in Dunkin Donuts staring at the ceiling; thinking of what courses I will take to start my writing career, when this guy walked in. He was gorgeous, tall, blond hair, with blue eyes, and I *think* if I am not mistaken, he looked like Ryan Gosling; his hair just glowed in the light.

He saw me staring at him and he smiled. He bought his cup of coffee and sat next to my table. It was a funny scene. While I thinking about my future I was also thinking about my heart. With every sip from his cup of coffee, he was looking in my direction. He watched me reading through each course. He was fascinated by the way I was sitting in my chair and how I was observing my books.

At that moment, he got up from his chair and came to my table. I was quivering in excitement with every step he took towards me. When he approached my table, he sat on the chair and gazed into eyes. He was looking at me. He was *really* looking at me, as if he wanted me to answer his eyes with a glimpse of mine. I tried my best not to look at him but I could not resist his intent glance. I looked at him and smiled.

At that moment he got up once more and bought me a cup of coffee. I said, "Thank you." "You're welcome." He replied. We sat there for a few hours talking about anything; but how gorgeous he is. He was so interested in getting to know me. Without hesitation, I spoke about myself. *My name is Anna. I am eighteen years old. I want to be a writer. I love going out and making new friends. I never had a boyfriend. I have only one friend. She is my best friend actually. Her name is Jill.*

Subsequently, he spoke about himself; his name is Mike Jenkins. He is eighteen years old. He is a street racer. He has a fascination for strange places and is a risk taker. I really liked him a lot and felt that we connected;

astoundingly, he felt the same way and asked me out. *I am so in love.* I thought to myself while staring at him with relief and happiness.

At first, though, I said no, because my parents have this image of me, and well his image as a street racer, I mean, is not quite a number one image for a boy they wish their daughter to be with, let along, date him. They have this certain idea of a guy-type for me and well, I love my parents and everything, but come on, there is no Mr. Right lurking round my corner any time soon.

I thought about it another time and wondered, *what was bad about dating a street racer?* Finally, I accepted the offer of to go out with him of course without getting permission from my parents first. I mean, *come on*, and *look at him*! He is gorgeous and I would be stupid if I miss an opportunity to go on a date with Mike Jenkins. I agreed and made sure he knew and understood I *never hook up easily.*

After a while sitting in the coffee shop, we said our goodbyes and left. I went home, said hi to my parents and ran upstairs to my bedroom. I was so excited with meeting Mike that I opened my diary and scribbled feelings felt for Mike. While scribbling, my phone rang. It was a text message. I received a text message from him, Mike Jenkins:

Anna was rly plzd I met u. I think, I like you. I knw we'll b gr8 2getha.

I read it. I read it again. I read it another time. I was happy that he acknowledged the flirt that happened at the coffee shop. I was not so sure that he would send me a text message but he did. I was excited that I replied quickly, without hesitation, a simple text message:

**Mike. I think I like you, too. I am happy to have met you.
See you soon. ☺**

After I send my text, I was eagerly waiting for a reply, but, I did not receive another text. I was a bit disappointed because I was expecting to have an evening of chatty texts that we could be like those *couples* who text for hours and end the night with goodnight and sweet dreams, like in the movies.

Despite my disappointment, I called my best friend Jill. We have been friends since we were three years old. She did not go to the same school I loathed. She went to public school. I told her about my encounter with Mike. At first, she was uneasy about me dating a street racer as my first boyfriend. She then said that I should be extra careful, also I should not be over excited about him. However, she was still happy that I met someone, and on my own. At times I feel that we get each other and at other times, I just want to stuff food down her throat because she annoys me too much.

Jill is very outgoing and fun. She is the type of girl that does not have home or sleep in her agenda. She is full of life and makes me feel alive and happy every day. My parents approve of her but at times they do not like her constant party plans. The next day, I woke up feeling a little blue. However, my mood changed when I saw a text message from Mike:

Goodmoro SUNSHINE!! Sry bout last night, I slept n just got up. I had a dream about u last night ☺. I dreamt u and I went for a romantic breakfast at the plaza n I took u 2da shopping mall. Now, how does that sound? ;)

I was baffled by his text. I was about to answer him quickly but I decided to confide in Jill. She told me to act natural and not to get too excited. I agreed and did just that:

Hello Mike. That is so sweet of you, but I kind of promised to be with Jill today. I am sorry. Can we make it another day instead?

For the past five minutes I did not receive anything from Mike, and then he sends me a text saying:

Anna, how bout dinner?

I was ecstatic. I also told Jill and she let me in on a little secret; *he may be nice, but, he may also be playing a little nasty game.* Then again, he is totally sexy and I would not dream of letting him go. I agreed to dinner with Mike.

Our first few dates were very plain and no excitement. I felt that he wanted to get to know me. He took me on fun dates. We went to the movies. We took long walks in the park. It was all very romantic and I was enjoying every minute of it. We did not do any physical interaction other than hand holding. I did not allow him to kiss me. I just felt shy. I never kissed a boy before. I felt that I was not ready for the kissing part of the relationship.

I introduced him to my parents and they loved him. After the meeting with my parents, he felt a little uncomfortable. He began backing out on a few things, such as dinner with my parents or even coming over to my place. He was a bit on edge because it all felt new to him. He did not want to lose his *manly* image that everyone knows him as. The problem I was facing was that I was falling head over heels for him day in day out. Nevertheless, I was feeling scared because he was my first boyfriend.

Our feelings for each other were like *bread and butter*. Together they make a good combination but separate, bread is dull without butter. We dated for two months. It was magical and a little bit like a fairy tale. I felt like I was a princess and I may have finally found my prince.

One cold, November night, 2002, I went to his house to surprise him with tickets to a Britney Spears concert. The funny thing about the concert was that it was a girl's thing but he liked going with me. His target was making me happy and he always accomplished that.

I won the tickets while answering a question on the radio. That was a bonus for our relationship that he did not need to buy the tickets. Sometimes money is an issue for us. I would object dating someone who has money problems, but, he does take me out and satisfies me so that is not a big deal.

I knocked the door and to my disclosure a girl answered the door wearing nothing but a t-shirt I bought for him. She was extremely sexy. She looked like one of those swimsuit models. She had long silky blond hair, shiny tanned skin and had a butterfly tattoo on her left ankle. I assumed she was his sister, because I have not met anyone in his family, yet.

He only met my parents and they loved him, very polite, sweet and down to earth. I may understand his issue with introducing me to his parents but his siblings might be another issue. How hard would it be to introduce your girlfriend to your brothers and sisters, unless you have something to hide from your girlfriend? Despite that idea in my mind, he said the blond girl, "Sexy, who is at the door," I looked at her in shock. For a while, I was standing there and could not move. She looked at me and said, "are those for me?"

"Hello? Any one in there? Are those tickets for me?" She asked me again while trying to get me to talk to her; let along say something.

"I am sorry I have the wrong house." I replied while giving her the tickets and left his house.

I ran so fast. I got into my car and drove away. I was driving away so fast. I was driving like a street racer. Now, isn't that ironic? I never did that before and yet, the feeling of pressing the paddle and speeding with the ache of my heart was sort of like pleasure and excitement. *What was I thinking? Of course a guy like him wants something. He is a street racer for God's sake. He is into the physical stuff more than the hugs. I cannot believe I was that stupid to believe he would stay away from it for me.*

After driving like a crazy person, I went straight home, ran up to my room, closed my door and cried on my pillow. I cried my eyes out. I was just too shocked that this happened to me. I watched so many movies and never in my life pictured it would happen to me. He came out and asked the girl again, "Who was at the door?" He was flabbergasted when the first question he asked she did not say anything. He looked at her and she was flipping her hair left and right. Then, she saw his hesitation and replied with ease.

"Some chick with tickets in her hand; she gave them to me; she seemed sad though when she left."

"Wait . . . what?" He wondered for a bit who could the girl be and then figured out that I was at his door.

"Yes, Mike, a girl was at the door. Who is she?"

"My girlfriend . . ." He answered hoping I still am.

"I thought you did not have a girlfriend." She said with a disappointed tone of voice.

"I do, or did . . . listen, wait here and I will be back."

He got dressed and was heading for the door when the girl stops him.

"Mike, I might not be here when you get back."

"Do what you want to do, but I must go."

He grabbed his keys and left the girl standing there. She was feeling a bit guilty at what happened. Although, it was not her fault because he tricked her in doing what he wanted with his super charms. She got dressed and left his house, with the Britney tickets in her hands.

He was calling me non-stop. He even sent me text messages telling me that he wanted us to talk. I told my parents to tell him that I did not want to talk to him. They tried their best to do what I asked for but then told him to be honest with me and tell me what he wants us to be. I allowed him to come up and *talk*. I was so mad at him that I felt like throwing him out of the window.

He took me in his arms and said, "What you saw is not what you *saw*."

"Then, what was it, Mike?"

"I love you, Anna."

"You must be joking. I was wondering when I was going to hear those words from you, I did not know that I had to see you with another girl to actually hear them."

"Anna . . . I really love you, I do. However, we have been dating for two months and you have not even kissed me, I feel that you do not love me."

"Do not dare turn to this around on me? I will not allow you to say this. Of course I love you, but what I saw is not what I was expecting to see, but I saw it and I will not accept it. You became my boyfriend accepting the consequences. I told you I do not hook up easily. You made sure that for our sake you would sacrifice the one thing you cannot be away from, but you did not; so . . . what do you think should happen now?"

"Anna, guys need a few things these days and well, if they do not get it from their girlfriend's, they . . ."

"Get it from porn." I smirked at him with angriest frown on my face.

"No . . . hmmm, ehhh, they get it . . . from sluts."

"Mike, I never want to see you again."

"Anna, please, I love you." He kneeled on his knees and begged me to forgive him but I was so mad that I did not want to hear another word.

"Shut up! You are a liar and a cheater and a liar and I hate you and it is over!"

He got up and pleaded to hug me and come close to say that he wants to be with me, also he tried his best to keep me in his arms and stated, "Anna, please . . . I am sorry." I pushed him away from me and out of my room. I sat on my bed in tears. They came out like a fountain of disappointment. I was devastated at what happened. I did not deserve that. Why did he do that? Why would he say the *L* word at a time when he was caught doing something wrong?

He left my house feeling guilty as ever. He went to his house hoping at least he could find that girl he was with and she was not there, either. He just went to bed feeling sad but tired from trying to convince me that the choice he has made was a guarantee. That was the last time I saw him. I tried to forget him in many ways. I tried writing about him. I tried talking about him. Although, none of those things I was trying to fill my time with would allow me to forget him. They made me want him more and more. I could never forget him. It was hard and painful; but, I had to let go. I was expecting him to come back to me but the reality was that he was gone. Jill warned me about him but I did not listen to her. I wish I did. At least I did not go any further then I would have really regretted it.

It was hard for a few months. All I could do was write my feelings away. I cried and I ate, but I never picked up the phone to call him though deep inside I wanted to just crack. Jill supported me through the whole problem I was facing and I was very grateful. It just seemed really hard and I wished he would just call me.

I honestly know that a two month relationship is not that difficult to overcome. He was my first boyfriend and he was what I thought was a pure real love and I f ell for him very quick. He was not and that is what is hard to forget. The first hand holding experience and long walks in the park; that was hard to forget.

Surprisingly, on February 6th, 2003, *Mike* called me. I felt amazed. I did not imagine that he would call me after how we ended it. I let the phone ring. After fifteen minutes on the dot, my phone rang again. I let the phone ring some more. Another fifteen minutes, the phone rang a third time. I decided to answer and for some reason I did not want to but I *answered,* anyway.

"Hello," I said.

"Anna?" Mike asked.

"Yes." I replied.

"How are you?" He asked.

"I am fine, thanks, yourself?" I said.

"Great." He stated.

"Good." I gathered.

We did not talk for a few seconds. I think he felt guilty of what he did to me that he was calling to apologize. It was late though because it has been three months since we spoke. I am still mad at him and there is no way I will take him back. Despite my feelings for him, it was *better late than never, right?*

"Anna." He says.

"Yes Mike . . . ?" I asked.

"What are you doing on Friday, February 14th?" He asks.

"Valentine's Day? So far nothing, although I do feel that I need a little *alone* time, but what do you have in mind?" I replied.

"You *do not* have a boyfriend?" He asked in shock.

"*No* . . . why . . . Do you have a girlfriend?" I replied again, with ease.

"Yes . . ." He stated.

"Awkward."

What was I thinking? Why did I answer the phone? I should tell him that I do not want to hang out with him and his girlfriend. I should tell him I do not want to see him. I should tell him some silly excuse and close the phone, now.

"Mike."

"Listen, before you object, there is a party on Friday, February 14th. I have a friend who is on his own, too. He just broke up with his girlfriend. I thought about you assuming you are single and I hoped you'd be. We are all friends at the end of the day and the girl you saw the other night at my house, well, we are dating now. She is my girlfriend and she told me to invite you. If you do not come I will assume you still love me and we cannot be friends. Come and hang out with my friend. It will be fun. Cool?"

"Wow . . . I will think about it." I replied with a cocky voice.

"I hope you come . . . do not take this in the wrong way, okay, but . . . I miss you."

Those words made me weak at the knees. I cannot believe he said he misses me. How could he miss me and be with another girl?

"Mike, about Friday, I am in. On one condition though, is he cute?"

"He is better looking than me."

"It is settled, then."

"One more thing, though, do you miss me at all?"

"You know I do."

I told him goodbye and I hung up the phone. I should have said nothing, but instead, I acted like a weak person and blurted out my feelings. He sort of knew my feelings for him but went along with his question so that I could admit it to him. That made him feel better and more confident because of his feminine outburst of saying that he misses me. I called Jill and she came over to talk to me about the phone conversation. Jill and I have no siblings so we consider each other as sisters.

"Anna, listen to me very carefully. I am your sister and I care about you but I do not trust Mike. He sounds sly and like he is up to something." Jill mentioned.

"What are you talking about, Jill?" I asked.

"Listen, you are a very sweet yet vulnerable girl and guys like Mike take advantage of that and they make it their priority to nail and bail. Since Mike has not succeeded in what he was trying to do to you when you were together I think he will send his friend to do that to you, now. Be smart and strong and show him who is boss! You are the boss and it is up to you how to go, where to go and when to go. Okay?" Jill explained.

"How do you know all this Jill?" I asked.

"Anna, we have seen all of them in movies but I do not think you paid any attention to any of the movies we have seen together." Jill continued.

My instincts about the party were very dodgy. I doubted my decision but I really wanted to show him that I do not care. My actions I had to take were decided upon how the reaction was held in Mike and his friend's direction. Though I was sure that there was an entity of nail and bail policy, I also felt that maybe he was genuine and doing the blind date out of the goodness of his heart. Jill did not believe the heart part because of what happened with the blond girl at his house, so I took caution.

February 14th Friday 2003 arrived quickly; half an hour before I join Mike, his girlfriend and his friend at the Valentine's bash. I was looking at myself in the mirror. *Any final touches*, I thought to myself. I am tall, I have long straight, black hair, hazel eyes and I am wearing a short red dress with black heels and I am holding a cute Chanel black bag. I was very anxious and eager at the same time but I felt convinced that I was going to have fun. Jill picked out my outfit and she even did my hair.

I called Mike and told him I was on my way. He told me to go to his house so we could all leave together. I agreed. I arrived at his house and knocked the door. I was anxious and excited because I wanted to see his reaction to my *new* look.

He answered the door and was so traumatized when he saw me; *gorgeous* he thought to himself. He was mad that he arranged all this but kept his anger intact. He never saw me *girlie* myself up like this and he was very pleased. He took my hand and kissed it. I smiled at him and walked in.

He was not done yet. He took me to his living room and introduced me to his girlfriend and his friend. We sat in his living room. His girlfriend Sally and his friend Jason were both staring at me. it was a great moment for me. I was feeling sexy and powerful. It was a great thing that I went to his house. After a few minutes, I got up off the couch and said, "Are we not going to party?"

Mike came out of his room and looked at me. I began walking for the door. Sally got off the chair as well and came with me. We waved to the boys and said bye. Jason got up grabbed Mike and followed us. We went in one car. His friend Jason is extremely attractive; Jason is tall, also, dark hair and brown eyes; Jason looked like Channing Tatum. Jason and I sat in the front seats and Mike and Sally sat in the back seats.

It took us around fifteen minutes to arrive at the party. On the way, no one spoke a word in the car. We were looking around and listening to the music playing in the car stereo; the song that was playing was differences by Genuine. The funny incident that happened was that my heart was thumping extra hard and I assumed that they could hear it but no one could. We arrived at the party; Jason was looking for a parking place. He dropped us at the door and told us to go in. It was loud and crowded.

We sat at our table Mike reserved for us. He reserved it like a month ago without knowing my answer; he still reserved. It felt like this whole thing has been planned just like Jill and I were discussing. It did not feel really weird but weird was the right word for the feeling I was having towards this whole night. Finally, Jason came after parking the car. It took him a while. It looks like he parked it very far away that he literally had to walk back to the party. He sat beside me. Mike ordered a bottle of champagne for the table.

After ordering, he whisked Sally by her hand and took her to the dance floor. I kind of got jealous because I was expecting him to ask me to dance despite her being his girlfriend. I could not stop looking at them. He looked better than ever and I hated to admit to myself that I missed him so much. Mike knew I was looking at him and he ignored me. Jason, on the other hand, would not stop looking at me. He asked if I wanted to go for a walk. Outrageously I agreed. We passed by Mike and Sally and left the party.

The sky was clear. No clouds in sight, just beautiful bright stars. It was very romantic and I felt like I was in a movie at that moment. I was shaking a bit from the cold so Jason offered to give me his jacket and I accepted. *A true romantic if you ask me.*

"Are you okay?" asked Jason.

"Yes, why do you ask?" I replied.

"You were staring at Mike and paid no attention to me." He stated.

"I am so sorry . . . I did not mean to do that."

"Anna, listen, I am sorry for intruding. You do not want to be here with me, correct? I feel that I have a competition with Mike."

"What do you mean?"

"Well, the way you are staring at him is very hard because I cannot stop looking at you."

"He was my boyfriend. He is your friend. How could this work? It cannot work."

"To be honest, Mike never said anything about you being his ex-girlfriend. He just told me you are friends."

"What?" I asked in disappointment.

"How old are you?"

"What do you mean friends?"

"Oh, I did not mean to insult you or anything, but he did not say you were together. He just said you hung out a few times that was it . . . sorry."

"Hung out, is that what he called it???!!" I ranted.

"Why are you annoyed?"

"I am irritated . . . I just do not get how he could say he loves me and he told you that we just *hung out*? Anyway, I am nineteen years old and yourself?"

"He said the *L* word?"

"Yes, he said the *L* word. What is so hard to believe?"

"Mike is the type where he has to mean to say *I love you*; no offence Anna."

"None taken . . ."

"Enough of Mike; how old are you?"

"I told you, I am nineteen years old and yourself?"

"Same."

I hated what I heard. It made me hate Mike more and more. I was feeling that my time I wasted with him was really unreal and my effort to loving him was counterfeit. I cannot believe that he told Jason we just hung out. I cannot believe he told me he loves me. How can he do that to me? Why did he do that? Why did he say that he misses me when it was all fake? I hate him for making me have feelings for him.

Jason and I were getting along really well. I wanted to *kiss* Jason. I really wanted to revenge on Mike but I also wanted to be with Jason. I was also confused about my whole situation that I had to calm down. I could not because I was nervous and excited, confused and happy, frustrated and safe, all in the same moment.

"Anna, I think we should go out?"

"You mean like on a *date*?"

"Yes why not?"

"I do not think so."

"Why not?"

"I do not know anything about you."

"That is why it is called a *date*."

"Right . . ." I smirked.

"What do you say?"

"No."

"Why not . . . ?"

"I do not want to."

"Anna . . . I like you and I know you like me, so, what is the problem?"

"Mike."

"What about Mike?"

Jason and I were a perfect match for each other. We both love writing and going on adventurous trips and watching movies. Mike was nothing like Jason. While getting to know Jason a friend of Mike's was outside talking on the phone when he saw us. He heard a bit of the conversation that he ran in to tell Mike. He told him that we were communicating about our first date.

Despite Mike introducing Jason to me, he got mad. He did not assume that I would get cozy with Jason. He did not want the cozy part to happen but it did. Subsequently, he thought of making the night more interesting for his ego. Mike left Sally on her own on the dance floor and went out to stop the *date* from happening.

"I thought you were my friend, Jason." Mike blurted.

"What are you talking about, Mike?" He asked.

"I gave you *permission* to go out with her tonight only and this is how you repay me."

"Wait a minute here Mike; you told him I was just a friend of yours so what is the problem if we do go out?" I interrupted.

"Shut up!" He exploded at me. I looked at him in disgust and slapped him in his face. He pushed me on the floor. I fell down and hurt myself after that he punched Jason in his face. He said, "You are not worth my time at all, not you or her." He went back to dancing with Sally.

Jason got up and helped me up. I tried my hardest to dust the mud off myself. He offered to drive me to my car. I accepted. We said nothing in the car, on the ride to my car. We arrived at my car, were sitting in his car in shock and disbelief of what just happened with Mike. Jason told me he was going back to the party to see what exactly happened because it was all weird.

"I feel so responsible." I said.

"Why? It is not like you punched me." Jason said.

"I know, but still, if I did not come to the party, none of this would have happened." I mentioned.

"No, Anna, if you did not come to the party, I would not have met you."

"Jason, that is sweet but . . ."

"But, what . . . ?"

"I do not feel ready."

"Ready for what? We are not going to get married. It is just a date. If you feel, at any time, that we are not good for each other, tell me and I will never speak with you again."

"Jason . . ."

"Honestly, Anna, I like you."

"I . . ."

Jason took my hand and hugged me. I pushed him away in confusion. He was shocked.

"What was that for?"

"Jason . . ."

"Yes . . ."

"You just got punched . . . in *your* face . . . by *your* friend."

"What is your point?"

"I do not mind hurting you, too."

"Anna, listen, I like you . . ."

"Jason . . ."

"What?"

"Nothing . . ."

"Anna, can I ask you something?"

"Yes."

"Have you ever been *touched*?"

"Are you *out of your mind* asking me this question?"

"Anna, I asked you if anyone has *touched you* not if you are *still a virgin*, which seems to me, *you still are*. Have you?"

"Have I what?"

"Been touched?"

"No."

"Has Mike kissed you?"

"No."

"Can I kiss you?"

Before I could object, he kissed me and our lips passed saliva. It was a nice, sweet and tender kiss. I had butterflies in my stomach. I liked it. He kissed me again and tried to do more but I stopped him. He stopped with ease. He agreed to take it slow and that slow is better and safer for the both of us. He waited until I got inside my car. I fell on my bed and felt like I might have actually found *Mr. Right*. Although, Mr. Right does not always mean that the kiss is the key to Mr. Right. I just loved it, and I wanted to kiss him again and again and again and again and *again*.

After Jason waited for me to get into my car, he went back to the party. He was looking for Mike and found him making out with Sally in a corner. He asked to talk to him on his own. Mike did not want to listen to him at first, because he was busy with Sally and enjoying his make-out moment, but after he got interrupted by Jason he agreed to talk with him. He was really mad at him and was not supposed to be because it was his plan. He did not know the jealous rage he was going to have from this issue, though.

"Why did you punch me?"

"I do not know why. I got pissed you two made out."

"Made-out? Where did you hear that? Mike, if you do not want me to date her, just tell me."

"No. I do not mind. She is a great girl and I am fine with you two dating."

"You sure? Why did you not tell me you told her you loved her?"

"I do not know why. Maybe because of my image everyone has of me. I am a heart breaker and not a heart lover."

"Mike, please be honest with me, you are my best friend. Do you mind if Anna and I date?"

"Do you like her?"

"She is very sweet and my type of girl, man."

"Fine, then, it is cool with me."

"Okay, so, it is safe to say that I kissed her."

"You . . . kissed . . . her? When were you planning to tell me that?"

"Well, I just did."

"Listen, you and I are great friends. We will always be friends. She was my girlfriend and I did love her, but I would not mind you two dating."

"Great. I am glad you feel cool with this."

"Me too; but please do not hurt her in any way she does not deserve it."

"I know man. I really think I have feelings for her man. It is crazy."

"I am glad, Jason!"

"Well."

"What?"

"Mike?"

"Yes Jason?"

"Nothing . . ."

"Okay."

Their conversation ended. Five months passed, Mike grew more and more jealous of Jason and I. Mike and I no longer spoke. Jason and I became closer and developed into an official item. We would see each other every day. We were at either my house or his. I met his parents and they loved me. he met my parents and they loved him. We spoke for hours on the phone. We would go on adventurous trips together. We would watch movies and go to the theatre.

I fell in love with him and he was falling in love with me. When we kiss I would feel the kiss tingle all over my body and so would he. He would make me feel things on parts of my body. One night in August 2003, my parents were out to dinner, I texted Jason to come over. I was in my black dress but I did not think of wearing a bra. He came over wearing his yellow

Hawaii shorts and a White t-shirt. He brought the movie *Cruel Intentions* because he knew that I was a big fan of Ryan Philippe. I did not know what the movie was about because I have not seen it before. Once it started, I realized he was trying to tell me something with this movie. *Anna, definitely he wants sex.* I thought to myself.

We made popcorn and sat on the couch next to each other. The movie was all ups and downs until the scene between Ryan Philippe and Reese Witherspoon; having sex, got us excited. I enjoyed watching Ryan get all sweaty while having sex with every other girl in the movie. He is my favorite actor and I admired his sexy body. Jason sensed I was excited too that he came closer to me and put his arm around me. I looked at him and he made sure I was concentrating on him when he took his right hand and reached down for my boob. He moved in for the kiss so I would not realize that he was massaging my boob but I jumped up out of the couch and demanded that he left.

"Anna, are you kidding me?" Jason was shocked with my outrageous burst and did not leave until he made me realize that I wanted it too.

"What are you on about?" I asked.

"Are you telling me you did not like that?"

"I did."

"Then what was wrong?"

"The way you did it."

"Anna, we have been dating for five months; five wonderful months, I am entitled to a little boob action at least."

"Excuse me?"

"Okay, it came out wrong."

"Listen, Jason, you have to leave."

"Why did you wear a dress with no bra? What did you expect me to do when I saw your nipple go hard? You wanted me to ignore it?"

"Oh my God; you are really such a guy!"

"Duh; you knew that when we began dating!"

"I wore what I wore because knowing you are my boyfriend and feeling comfortable with you I did not expect to protect my body from being touched by you. Jason, we are together; that does not mean that I must hide myself from you and that does not entitle you to touch me without my permission. Did you not think of it that way?"

"Anna. I am sorry but you are too uptight! I really like you and I want to be with you, but not just the intellectual part of you. I want all of you!"

"Just not tonight, Jason! I was expecting just to sit and cuddle with my boyfriend trying to be comfortable with my body around you before we do anything further."

"Right, okay, you want us to cuddle more and me not get excited when I see your nipples get excited. Right . . . That may be normal to you but not for me, but as you like I will leave you alone."

He left. He made me feel guilty. I did not mean to make the relationship end like this. Although I did not feel it ended because he called me after he left; he apologized anyway. Even if we kissed and he may have been right about the boob action but I was not ready. Maybe if we dated a little longer then yes.

After our mess up a month ago, Jason became more understanding and he made me fall in love with him. I know six months is not a long time to love someone but I do. My parents met him and they also loved him, but my mother had her doubts about him. I will not blame her; she has those motherly vibes that I respect and trust.

One cool afternoon on Sunday 3rd September 2003, Jason called me to invite me over for our six month anniversary. At first I felt weird and declined. Then he asked me if I loved him, I said I do and then he insisted that I should go to his place. His place was scented with vital oils and his room was lit up with candles. There were red rose petals on his bed and in the bath tub, as well as, essential oils and also red rose petals on the surface of the water. I walked in wearing a silk purple dress above the knee with pleasant purple heels. My hair was neatly coiferred to the left side of my shoulder.

He was wearing a white t-shirt and black shorts. He looked amazing. He took me by my hand and kissed my lips. We held each other for a little while. We were slow-dancing to the wind. He mentioned to me that our six month anniversary was not about having sex, but about touching each other so that we would be comfortable when being with each other. He kissed me again; then he took his t-shirt off. He picked me up and put me on his bed. He slid my purple dress off my shoulders and began caressing my arm up and down; I lay on his bed; we were kissing. He gazed into my eyes and told me he loves me! I smiled and said it back.

He then got on top of me and we were rubbing up against each other. He was moving up and down rubbing our bodies against each other. I felt his body over me and I grabbed his butt and squeezed it hard from the excitement I was feeling. At the same time while I was squeezing his butt, he managed to massage my breasts gently allowing me to feel the sexual pleasure while doing so.

Suddenly, his phone rang; Mike was on the phone. "Hello." He said in a hesitating voice.

"Jason . . . what on *earth* are you doing?" Mike asked in disapproval.

"Well, I am with . . . ehhh . . . my girlfriend . . . What do you want?"

"Hi Mike." I stated.

"*Anna*?" Mike asked.

"Yes, Mike. I am Anna; can we help you with something?"

"Are you going to have sex?" Mike asked.

"It is none of your business man;" replied Jason while still rubbing our bodies against each other.

"Piss off Mike, we are busy!" I insisted.

"Jason, I want to remind you of our bet . . . ." He stated.

"Bet?" I gasped while looking at Jason.

I pushed him off me, got dressed up and headed for the door. He approached me; I slapped him and left his house in tears. Jason grabbed his phone and swore at Mike.

"Mike, what the hell is wrong with you? Why would you say that?"

"What happened?"

"She left. Why did you say that?"

"That was for kissing my ex-girlfriend and dating her. You said it the night you met her. We are best friends and best friends do not go out with their exes. That just a little pay back I was planning. Well, anyway, I better go now."

"Why would you do that when you said it was okay that we both date?"

"I said it was okay, but I did not mean it and you should have known. I arranged the date but not intentionally for you to ask her out."

"You are weird."

"Jason, do you love her?"

"Of course I do you, asshole. You have to call her up and tell her you were joking."

"Nah man, she will come to you dude, I am sure she will."

"No she will not. Pick up the phone and call her!"

"Okay. Do not be such a panzie." Mike replied.

Mike closed the phone and called me. I did not pick up the phone. Then Mike messaged me and told me that what he said was true and he wanted to tell me before but did not know how to tell me because he feared he was going to betray his best friend. At first, I did not believe him then; I thought about it a bit more and replied back saying that I believed him and I knew how to deal with Jason.

At that moment, Jason sat hesitantly waiting for Mike's response. Mike called him up and told him what happened. The thing is that Mike retaliated because we kissed in front of him and began dating and we actually fell in love with each other. This retaliation was not against me but against Jason and to teach Jason a lesson.

"Jason, she is not listening to me. She thought we were playing her. I do not know what to tell you, bro."

"Mike; do not make me come and tear your face apart."

"Jason you had it coming to you man."

"Do you still love her?"

"No, I do not. I am in love with Sally. Please believe me that I tried everything okay."

"Fine . . ."

He closed the phone in Mike's face. He got dressed and drove to my house. I was not at home. I went to Jill's house. I was in tears and I threw up twice. She called my parents and told them to tell Jason to leave me alone because it was over between us. He arrived at my house begging to explain that what Mike was playing a sick game and he was not part of it and did not mean for anything to happen and he was in love with me. My parents did not believe him and closed the door in his face.

He called my phone and it took him to voice mail. He left many messages apologizing but Jill told me not to look back. What was said was said. I listened to her. She drove me home and I took a shower and went to bed. I was so mad and irritated that I decided to make my feelings for Jason die. The feelings were too much for me to handle.

He tried to apologize many times on behalf of Mike and he tried so hard to get me back. He sent me flowers and gifts. He dedicated songs for me on the radio. Jason tried his best to say sorry for what was said during our romantic session but he was not getting anywhere with me.

I should have waited. Instead I allowed Jason to touch me. I allowed his hands on my body and his lips on my lips; I allowed his body to rub against mine and mine to rub against his. I allowed him to massage my breasts and make me sexually excited. Now I know the feeling of sexual excitement but I feel ashamed for giving in so quickly and not waiting for the real thing!

It took me exactly two months to get over my relationship that I experienced. I allowed myself to cry and feel weak and insecure. It was good for me because it made me grow and empower the existence of why I am here. I am here to explore the every part of my life from sadness to happiness, in order for me to be a great writer. After the two months of cleansing, I began this new ritual where I face the sadness and avoid my tears.

Ten months later, I paid more attention to myself and gave up on guys in general. I tried my best to keep my mind occupied and write but it was no use I was too blocked to make an effort. My parents insisted I spend more times with them. I hardly went out and if I did it was with Jill either to a shopping mall, gym or to the cinema. It was a plain and relaxed life.

That year I turned twenty; it passed without a word from Jason; he basically stopped his efforts to getting me back; I was glad he did that. That meant he was accepting that we were through. I was lonely but I felt that I was not ready to see anyone who could hurt me like Mike and Jason hurt me. Jill would make me laugh whenever I was trying to forget what happened between me and Jason and also make me smile; we even travelled together.

On Thursday 7th October 2004, Jill called me and told me about this hot party that she was invited to and wanted to take me with her. At first, I declined, then, I thought to myself *I need some fun in my life*, so I agreed. She came over and we got ready to have fun. We looked elegant but I did not feel that way. We arrived at the party. There were a lot of people there. She met up with her friends. I sat in a little corner, pouting, by myself.

Suddenly, a young lad was approaching me. He was tall, dark hair and handsome; not the ugly handsome, but the gentleman type handsome; he looked like Josh Duhamel. He was coming towards me; my insides began tingling down my spine . . . I never felt that feeling before. It was funny yet exciting and I felt maybe the young lad, who was coming *my way*, maybe he wanted to *chat*.

Unpredictably, he walked right passed me and went to his group of friends that were sitting in a corner near me. I was really shocked that I got up and went to Jill. She looked at me in a weird way and told me that I should be out of my mind if I left the club and not talk to him. She told me I should make a move because he might be shy. I thought about it for a bit, and then marched up to him.

"Hey, how are you?" I asked with a shiver in my voice.

"I am fine, thank you." He said politely while he was looking around the club paying no attention to me.

" . . . Okay, I am sorry to bother you." I said politely and went back to Jill.

I told Jill I was leaving and she begged me not to go.

"Jill, I made a fool of myself, thank you for your great advice."

"Anna, please stay a while longer. Come on, wait for him, he will come to you, I am sure."

"No. I am leaving now." While I was talking to Jill, the boy came to me and stood behind me.

"Anna, turn around."

"Why should I? It is not like he is standing behind me . . ."

"Think again." Jill told me.

I turned around and I saw him standing there. He grabbed my hand and pulled me on the dance floor. I felt like I was on the moon. We were dancing hip-hop, jazz and salsa together. I could not believe myself. I was actually having fun again. After all this time I was having fun. Jill so that I was enjoying myself, she went home without me. I received a text from her telling me that she had already left and she was sorry that she forgot me. The boy offered, "I could take you home, if you'd like?" I nodded my head. The funny thing is that, so far, of all the dancing, and flirting, I still do not know his name; we got into his car. He felt that I wanted to ask him for his name but did not because I might have been shy; he told me his name.

"I am Tom Kelly, by the way."

Then, he drove to my house. He parked outside my house.

"I am Anna Swing." I replied.

"How old are you, Anna?"

"I am 20 and yourself?"

"22."

"What do you do, Anna?"

"I am a student at Snow Ville University."

"Okay, what do you study?"

"A bit of everything . . . I actually want to be a writer."

"Interesting . . . I study at Bridget Donnelley University. I am taking banking and financing courses and I still got a year and then I am done."

"Cool . . ."

"Listen, I do not mean to be forward or anything, but, I was wondering if you would like to go out on a date with me, let's say . . . Saturday night?"

"Sure . . . why not."

"Anna, I am glad we met each other and I admire how you came up to me tonight, which was pretty brave of you. I admire bravery in a girl. I felt really shy to talk to you because I thought you had a boyfriend."

"To be honest, after I came to talk to you, and I was ignored by you; I thought to myself *why the hell did I bother with that boy.* Do you know if you did not come back to talk to me, I would have left and well we could not have met."

"You are wrong there; we could have met anytime, even, if you left."

"How . . . ?!"

"I have seen you around."

"Where . . . ?"

"Here and there with Jill, but I was too shy to approach you."

"Oh . . ."

"Anna, I have passed through many girls in my life but none were as sweet and as fun as you were tonight . . . I promise you."

"I am truly flattered Tom . . . I really am."

"Have a nice evening, Anna."

"Bye, Tom, and thanks for the ride."

"Sweet dreams . . . Anna."

He kissed my hand softly. Butterflies hovered my stomach. He got out of the car and approached the passenger side door. He opened the door and walked me to my house door. He hugged me and again kissed my hand gently. I hugged him back and kissed his cheek. I waved goodbye. He waited until I got inside and then he drove off. I went up to my room. I lay swiftly on my bed and slowly went to sleep!

Saturday 16th October 2004, approached really quick. I was very nervous, because I was actually going on a *real date* where we have dinner and then party afterwards. I did not know what to do so I called Jill over to come over. She came with her essentials for a perfect outfit, for a date.

"Calm down . . ."

"I am calm . . . very calm . . . why would I not be calm?"

"Because you keep brushing the same side of your hair and I think you added a little extra fluff to it."

Jill did my hair and my makeup. She gave me a selection of outfits that would fit perfectly for tonight. There was a black set which was a black short dress until the knee with white accessories. There was a blue set which was a blue shirt like top with straight blue jeans skirt. There was a pink set and a red set which were both sporty yet classy t-shirts with white jeans. I chose the blue outfit because it looked sweet and elegant.

I looked at myself in the mirror and thought, *wow, I look gorgeous*. I sat in the living room with Jill and my parents. They told me I looked very attractive and that they were incredibly proud of me. It was 7:30pm and I was really nervous. I look at Jill and smiled. I was finally happy with myself and where I reached. I heard a car horn. It was Tom. I went outside and was surprised to see him early. He smiled at me, got out of his car and opened the door for me. *What a gentleman*, I thought to myself. I went close to him. We kissed each other on the cheek. We got into his car and drove off.

"You look beautiful, Anna," commented Tom while I was putting my seat belt on.

"Thank you, Tom . . . you do not look bad yourself."

He was dressed up also. He wore an exquisite, elegant suit he bought from Boss. It was navy blue with a white shirt. He looked extremely hot! I loved his choice of shoes that he wore with his well-designed suit; a suit with white trainers from Adidas. Sexy!

"Are you excited or nervous to be on a date with me?"

"I am not sure really, but I would like to know where you are taking me?"

"It is a surprise."

I was excited but a little scared because I did not know what to expect and if I was actually dressed for the occasion correctly. He put some music on. The music we were listening to was ballet-jazz with a slight touch of soul. It was pretty soothing. We did not say anything to each other the whole ride to the restaurant.

After our fifteen-minute drive, we arrived at a cozy restaurant. It was right near a club called *The Love Shack*. I asked Tom if we were going there next and he told me I should enjoy my meal and then think of our adventure tonight together.

We walked in and it was very warm. It was full of candle-lights and the waiters were dressed elegantly. The manager greeted us and told Tom, "Mr. Kelly, right this way sir, and just so you know everything is as you asked for. Have a nice evening sir, madam . . ."

We reached a round table with two chairs and a bottle of champagne. On the table were a dozen white roses with a card addressed to me. I looked at Tom and he told me I should read the card. I took the card, and read it. It said *this is to a wonderful night with a maiden of sworn beauty, a night you will never forget, nor will I. I am proud to say that I felt love at first sight when I first met you.* Romantic, yet cheesy, but I liked it. I gazed into Tom's eyes and smiled. He smiled back and we sat at the table.

Our dinner was wonderful and I could not have asked for a better night. After dinner, Tom told me that he had reservations at the Love Shack and we were expected to be there. I agreed and departed with him. I took my flowers with me. He offered to put them in the car and I accepted. Then, we went to the club.

At the club, people were dancing and screaming and going nuts to the music. I was scared because I felt that I might see the two people that I was not ready to see yet. Tom took me by my hand and we went to the VIP section. There was another champagne bottle and a dozen of *red* roses at the VIP section. I sort of understood what he was trying to say with the red roses, I was pleased.

After the Love Shack, he drove me home and we parked outside my house. He took me by my hand and kissed me on my neck then kissed me on my cheek then kissed me on my lips. To my shock, I did not stop him and I allowed him to continue. I kissed him back. After kissing each other for a while, he stopped and told me how much he feels that we should be together. I agreed and told him that I felt the same.

"Anna, from the first moment I saw you I knew that we would be great together."

"Tom, so do I."

"I believe we would be a smashing couple."

"I trust that, too."

Two months passed; Tom and I were inseparable. It was amazing. I felt that finally I could *give* myself to love. At long last, I could fall into love without any problems from my end. We would go every other night to the Love Shack. We have made it into our hang out spot. Everyone knew us there and we almost had everything to our disposal. The manager of the Love Shack gave us the VIP section for us. We basically owned it and did not have to reserve.

It is now January 2005, Tom and I were planning my birthday night out. We got dressed, had an early dinner at my place with my parents. Later, we went to the Love Shack and Jill came with us. There were a lot of people out tonight; old and new. Jason and Mike came with two different girls. We crossed eyes but did not say hi to each other. I went to the bathroom while Tom was ordering drinks for us.

I was coming out of the bathroom when I saw Jason, drunk as usual, standing outside; waiting for me. He was staring at me. He looked at me and said, "I have missed you so much and I do not know why." I smirked at him while saying, "I moved on Jason, so should you."

For a moment we were just standing there looking at each other. Then, he approached me and everything changed between us. I thought he was going to hug me but instead, he pushed me against the wall and began kissing me. I tried to push him off but he was too strong. He pulled my arms above my head and begins fondling places under my shirt that I hadn't allowed Tom to touch me yet. His hands worked their way down and inside my pants.

I screamed and kicked him between his legs and then, I fell to the ground in tears. I thought no one heard me because of the loud music but to my surprise Tom came to my *rescue*. "What is going on here?" Jason got up, looked at both Tom and I and then walked off. Tom approached me and I screamed again. I ran off leaving Tom shocked out of his mind for what happened.

For a few seconds I was out on my own. At that moment, Tom came after me. We were standing outside trying to decipher what had just happened. He was looking at me and did not know what to say. I, on the other hand, did not want to say anything to him and began walking off with tears in my eyes. He came in front of me and stopped me.

"Anna, what is wrong?"

"Nothing . . ."

"Who was he?"

"No one . . ."

"Anna, what did he do to you?"

"Tom, I just want to be alone."

"Why?"

"Tom, I just want to be on my own."

"Do you love him?"

"No . . . ! I am going home."

"Let me take you."

"No."

"Why?"

"I want to be alone."

"Anna, please . . ."

"Tom, please leave me alone."

I was walking off when he called me again and said, "Anna, I love you."

That did it. He had to say that? I did not reply and I just went home. He did not know what he said wrong he just stood there staring at me while I was walking off. He just expressed his love to me and all I did was walking off; can you blame me? I have been through two break ups and both boys said *I love you*. The one person who deserved my respect and love. I just threw trash in his face, was Tom.

After, he went back to the party, he told Jill everything. She opened up to him. She believed he was in love with me. She told him the story that there once was *Jason and I*. He asked her a few questions and she told him all he wanted to know. He did not feel that it was right for me to leave like that but he let it be the way I wanted.

"You are telling me that he still loves her, and might have touched her in any way or form?" asked Tom.

"I do not know what to say Tom, but yes, maybe that is what happened . . ." answered Jill.

I was at home in my room thinking about what Tom said. I thought to myself that I could not take back what happened but I could improve it. I called Jill and told her to tell Tom that I just needed some time on my own and I would be better soon. She did and he was okay with it. He told her to tell me that I could have all the time I needed and that he loves me no matter what.

A month passed and I was not feeling as I should be feeling. Tom and I were talking on the phone but we have not seen much of each other. It was not because of him, but of how I felt about the whole love cycle. I told him that I am happy with him but I need time to see who I am and who I am supposed to be. He agreed to give me time to myself. We did not break up. We are together but not going out together.

It is now Monday 6th February 2005; the beginning of the week. Today, I decided to see Tom no matter what because I felt I could not be without him anymore and I was sure he felt the same way. I got out of bed but was feeling a little dizzy. I felt like I was going to collapse. I went back to bed and rested for a bit. I called my mother who was at work and told her that I was not feeling well. She called my doctor and came home to take me there. On our way there, I was feeling weaker than ever.

At the doctors, we were waiting in the waiting room. My mother called my father and told him that she was with me at the doctors and that we would be a while. He did not mind and told her to call him if anything was serious. We waited for a while longer and I just got restless. I got up and suddenly collapsed to the ground. My mother screamed. The nurse came took me to the sickbay.

They were doing some tests. It took them a while to go through the results and everything was going smooth so far . . . My mother called my father and he rushed to the hospital. I was sleeping in bed and my parents were with the doctor who did the tests for me. He said that I had to stay in the hospital for a couple of days to make sure of what they found was true.

"What are you trying to say, doctor?" My mum asked in eagerness to know when I will leave.

"I think your daughter might have leukemia."

"What?" Asked my father.

"I am sorry . . . Although we do not know for sure, we need to do a few more tests to make sure."

My parents sat on the chairs traumatized; they came into my room and saw me awake. They did not want to scare me and told me I should stay in the hospital for a few days to see if my pressure will not rise again. They did not tell me I might have leukemia.

I told them that I wanted to call Tom and Jill to tell them where I am. They said that they did not want me to make myself uneasy. I must rest for my tests for the next couple of days. I did not buy anything they were saying to me and waited for them to leave and asked the doctor to tell me the truth.

"Anna you have Leukemia."

"What is *leukemia*?"

"Leukemia is cancer of the blood cells."

"Why do I have it?"

"We honestly do not know why you have it but you do. That is what is showing in your test results and I recommend you get treated immediately."

"Doctor, please explain to me very well what are you trying to say because I still do not get it."

"You are in shock dear. A girl, as healthy as you are has what has to be the worst problem a person can face but you do. Listen to me Anna, it is not a joke this cancer issue. You have to face that you have cancer and go about it as soon as possible. People who suffer from leukemia are at a drastically amplified risk for developing infections, anemia, and bleeding; such as other symptoms and signs which include easy bruising, weight loss, night sweats, and unexplained fevers. So you see what I am trying to tell you. It is very important we do something about it now."

"How long do I have doctor?"

"I assure you if we start chemotherapy you will be as good as new."

"Doctor that is not what I asked you; I asked you how long do I have?"

"Anna, for now, you are alive and you need treatment."

"Doctor, please answer me."

"I do not know how long you have, Anna, I am sorry."

"Come again?"

"I do not know dear."

I was speechless. The only thing, that was in my mind was, Tom. I could not stop thinking about him. My judgment of what I should do did not cross my mind. I told the doctor that I wanted to go home and I would decide on my own about whether I should have the treatment or not.

He told me I was foolish if I did not think of getting treatment. I then told him not to say anything to anyone and that I would see him in a week. He agreed and I went home. The next few weeks, I did not leave the house. I did not want to see or talk to anyone. I was in my room reading, writing, being on my own. I went again to the doctor with my parents and they were mad when they knew that I knew and I was told to do something about it and I declined.

"Did we deserve the silence?" My mother asked me.

I did not answer her. I just walked off. I thought my doctor promised he wasn't going to say anything. I was wrong, because my condition was becoming worse; by the second. One cool, early, Saturday evening, 26th February 2005, I went to the Love Shack. I was at the VIP section on my own. Then, I see a picture I did not dream of seeing at all . . . *Tom and Jill sitting, together, hand in hand*; I was in total shock, left my drink on the table and commenced on walking for the door, when Tom saw me and approached me.

"Where have you been?" He asked.

"In bed . . . Like you care . . ." I answered.

"Excuse me . . . I thought you did not want to see me and you wanted some time on your own . . ."

"It did not mean that we broke up."

"I know that."

"I do not think you do . . ."

"Do you mean, *Jill?*"

"Yes . . ."

"Jill asked me to help her with her *new* boyfriend, who happens to be my best friend and she called you once or twice and you would not pick up so she came to me."

"So . . . it is *my fault* now?"

"I am not saying that Anna, I am just trying to tell you . . . Anna, I have missed you so much."

I looked at Tom and smiled. His voice was cruising down my spine like I actually believed what he was saying. He was truly in love with me and not that *mumbo jumbo* kind of love. We hugged each other and I went to sit with them at their table. Jill hugged me and we began drinking together.

After a while, of having fun, I felt dizzy. Then I fainted on the table. Jill and Tom thought I was joking but, I did not get up. Jill called my mother and she told them to take me to the hospital. At the hospital everyone was outside my room except Tom. He was inside my room waiting for me to wake up. He was so mad at me. He could not believe that I did not tell him anything. He loves me and I should know what I am doing to him. He was really upset and actually left the room.

Jill came in and began talking to me. I could hear everyone talk, but I just wanted to listen. They deserved to talk to me since I turned them down. Tom was the only one who did not talk. Jill was blaming me for not telling her. She also blamed me for not telling Tom. *I understand how everyone is looking at the situation but I cannot be blamed for everything*, I thought to myself. *They should have made the effort if they really wanted to know about me and why have not I been in contact with them to make an effort to come and see if I was alright*, I thought again to myself.

Everyone once again left my room. Tom was still sitting on the chair. He was looking at me. He was not just looking at me but he was glancing at how I was laying on the bed and being helpless. Tom asked the doctors if he could stay with me for the night and they agreed since they were not going to send me home right away.

Two days passed, I was on my feet and ready to go home. Tom was not satisfied with what he heard and forced me to stay in the hospital for my treatment. I was angry with him and told him that he was insane but he did not care. He wanted to save me. He would do whatever it took to save me. I finally agreed because I love him and I did not want to disappoint him. He told me that he would be with me every day and he would never leave my side.

Four months passed, I went through a good treatment for a while. The doctors were optimistic about my recovery. I was skeptical. Tom was not sure what to believe and hoped that he did a good thing for me. It is now July 2005; it is hot. Tom asked if he could take me home and we went home. Jill was at my house with my parents. She was happy I was back home and she told Tom and me some good news about her *new* boyfriend and herself. They got engaged. I got a little jealous of her.

I wanted Tom to ask me to marry him, however, I was happy for her and I told her that we should celebrate. Tom was looking at me in a funny way. I did not know why he was looking at me in that way that I did not take his look into account.

"We can arrange a party another time, Anna," Jill stated.

"No . . . I may not have another time." I mentioned.

Tom did not like what I said and insisted on Jill that she should accept my offer just so that he would not hear another silly comment from me.

He was still mad at me. It has been four months but he is still mad at me because I did not tell him what I had found out. *He should forgive me if he loves me*, I thought to myself. Jill agreed with Tom and stated she wanted to do the party in August.

It is Monday 15th of August 2005; a very hot day. I went to get a bite to eat in the kitchen. To my surprise, I see everyone in the garden preparing brunch. They looked at me and began clapping. I had no idea of what was going on and went along with it anyway. Tom approached me and hugged me. We were hugging for a few seconds then I went around and hugged everyone else. Tom's family was there and so were Jill and her Fiancé. It was a beautiful day. I really enjoyed it.

Later that week, on August 27th, 2005, Tom, Jill, her Fiancé and I went to the *Love Shack*. We were having a well of a time. Suddenly, I see Jason and Mike dancing and they come along to say *hello*. They were in relationships too, and their girlfriends came with them. We were at our table drinking and dancing and having fun.

Jason apologized for his abnormal behavior a few months back. Mike apologized for not keeping in touch. It was an amazing night. We had a good time. I was feeling loved more by everyone and accepted despite having leukemia.

On October 7th, 2005, I was preparing myself to go to the mountains with my true love. Jason and Mike rented a cabin for us. Jill persuaded my parents to let me go with my true love. They arranged everything. Jason and Mike and Jill's Fiancé helped Tom with his *stuff* and Jill helped me with outfits to take on the trip.

The cabin was a two-hour drive away from civilization. I was excited and nervous at the same time. Tom was happy that he and I would be on our own, together, in a cabin in the mountains for a weekend. We arrived, after our two-hour drive, to the cabin in the mountains. We got settled in. It was cozy and had a fireplace too. It was like a studio-type cabin. It was basic open plan: kitchen and living room together with the fireplace, one bathroom, and one bedroom.

I loved it and so did Tom. We were proud to be friends with Jason, Mike and Jill. Subsequent to settling in, we went out into the woods. We walked for an hour and a half. We were just walking and observing nature. There was silence between Tom and I. We went back to the cabin. I went to have a shower while Tom was preparing dinner. He was cooking a dish his mother taught him before him and I came on this trip. He prepared my favorite. *Mexican!* It smelled wonderful. I, on the other hand, after I finished my shower, came out, wearing nothing but a towel. I felt like Tom and I were married and we were living on our own, forever. It felt so romantic. I went into our room and picked out a smashing set of clothes.

"Food is ready!" Tom announced.

The cabin was pretty warm so I wore something casual. We sat at the dinner table. It was brilliant. I loved every bite of it. After dinner, Tom and I washed the dishes together. Once we have finished the dishes, we brushed our teeth and I went to bed and Tom slept on the sofa.

He felt bad to sleep beside me on the bed. The reason for his decision was that; he and I did not experience the physical part of our relationship and he did not want to impose. That did not mean two people cannot sleep in bed together without *sleeping* together. Saturday morning, I woke up to breakfast in bed; charming and loving. He walked in with a red rose in his hand. He sat on the bed beside me. I smiled at him and took the rose from him. It smelled sweet and sensual. I was very happy. I was happier now, than I have ever been happy.

"I will clean the cabin a bit before we go on our hike. Finish your breakfast and get ready." Tom said with a smile on his face.

"Okay Tom, I would love to go on a hike with you." I responded.

After breakfast in bed, I went to the bathroom, washed up and brushed my teeth. While walking out of the bathroom I felt a sudden chill down my spine. I assume Tom may have left a window open in the living room; I then realized that a certain faint was approaching. I fell to the ground; thump!

Tom heard the noise and ran quickly to the room. He saw me on the ground and picked me up. He tried to wake me up. Nothing! Then, finally, after a few shoves and pushes, I woke up and I was startled by my own behavior. Tom suggested that I stay in bed to rest. I got upset because I was not tired anymore and I wanted to go out.

He objected and told me, "Once you feel better we will go for our hike, but please get better."

When Tom talks to me, he says it from his heart, which makes me so emotionally attached to him and want him more than ever. I agreed politely and asked him to do the same. He agreed. He at that moment went into the bathroom, had a shower and followed by that, he came to bed. We were both laying in the bed.

Tom, unexpectedly said, "Silence brings beauty out which you have not seen in your lover before."

"Smooth." I reply.

"Thanks . . . Anna, I want to spend my life with you."

"Tom, I love you and I want to be with you forever."

"We shall."

Subsequently, he got out of bed and into the living room. He came back and stood beside the bedside that I was laying down at. He knelt on one knee and said, "Anna, the first moment I saw you, I knew I wanted you, but I never knew I could have you. I love you with more moons and stars a person can dream of seeing. Close your eyes and imagine us together forever . . . Anna, will you marry me?"

"Oh my God! Tom . . . I do not know what to say . . ."

"Anna tell me what your heart is telling you."

"I love you Tom. My heart is telling me yes. Of course I will marry you."

He put the emerald ring on my finger. It was exactly like I expected. Finally, the one thing I wanted before I die. I marry the one I love. I kissed him on his cheek and he kissed me on my lips. We hugged each other for a while then I burst out, "make love to me Tom . . ."

"Anna, are you sure you want to do *it*, now?"

"Yes, what better time than now."

He took me by my hand and kissed me. He kissed my neck and I felt tingles down my spine and up my thighs. He then stopped, looked at me and smiled. We got into bed and we kissed each other again.

"Are you sure?" He asked me, still kissing me.

"Yes," I moan in excitement, "Tom . . . It is my first time."

"Do you want me to guide you?"

"Yes . . . if you do not mind."

"Why would I mind? I would be glad to guide you through this. You are my love. You are my life from now and on. I want to be with you forever."

"Tom, I cannot picture my life without you."

"Anna, I cannot either."

We began to undress one another; he caressed my thigh up and down, up and down . . . Then he massaged my left breast while licking the nipple on my right breast. It felt unbelievable and I cannot take the excitement too much. We removed all our clothes and were lying on top of each other naked in bed. I have never seen him naked. He looked so sexy. He moved in on me and worked his muscle *bone* in and out of my soft *sanctuary*. Tom and I were making love and it was the one time in my life I experienced love *and* pain at the same time. I was breathing heavily and so was he. He went fast and slow and I told him if I wanted it that way.

We made love without protection. I did not want him to use a condom or I did not ask him to. We were meant to be together and making love is part of being together forever. Tom wanted us to be together and so did I. Despite feeling that we should have used protection, it passed our minds because the one thing we did know was that we were getting married and that entitled us to start a family, so, we ignored the condom.

"Are you okay, Anna?"

"Yes Tom. I am having the time . . . of my life with you . . ." I said while breathing heavily.

"And I with you; my love . . ." He stated while panting.

"My heart is pounding really fast, is that normal?" I asked.

"It means you are in love."

"Are you in love?" I asked again.

"Yes."

The exhilaration I received from this was more energy filled than anything I have ever been through. To Tom's surprise I wanted to make love again. From Saturday night to Sunday afternoon, we had non-stop love making. It was energetic and exhausting at the same time. At 6:00pm,

Sunday afternoon, I received a phone call from my mother, "Anna, isn't it about time you and Tom head back home?"

"Yes. We will get ready and be on our way. See you soon. Mum, Tom asked me to marry him, by the way."

"What did you say?" She asked in excitement.

"Yes!"

"Great! Drive safe and come home to us, both of you!"

Tom called his mother also and told her that he asked me to marry him and that we were getting ready to leave. She also old us to come home safely. We tidied up the cabin plus got our things together. We were in the bedroom fixing the bed sheets when I pushed Tom on the bed and said, "Tom . . ."

"Yes Anna." He replied while kissing me on my neck.

"Make love to me . . . one last time . . . before we leave . . ."

"Why did you say *one last* time?"

"Well, I meant before we go home."

"Are you sure you did not mean because of your condition that you fear you will not survive."

"No, what does that have to do with what we been through this whole weekend."

"Are you sure? If that is the case I do not want to make love for the last time."

"No Tom, I love you and I swear I did not mean that. Will you make love to me, or not?"

"Okay, my Anna . . . Come here you sexy girl."

"Tom, I want all of you."

"And I you, my angel."

We made love another time, got dressed, did the bed and left the cabin. We drove for a while. There was a lot of traffic on the road. I was not comfortable with the traffic that I took Tom's hand and held it. He accepted to hold my hand and his fingers were caressing my fingers. Out of the blue, it began pouring with rain. Tom and I received messages from our mothers to drive safe on the road. It was 8:30pm and we were still on the road.

We reached a crossing. A lot of cars stopped to the side of the road. Tom felt he had to do the same but did not do what the others did. As an alternative, we continued our journey down the road. Unexpectedly, while driving safely down the road, a truck swerved out of its lane and into our lane. Tom and I saw it approaching us and we could not do anything about it. He just grabbed me and kissed me awaiting it to smash into us.

Our car flew in the air and it turned 360 degrees before it fell to the ground. It was still pouring with rain. The crash made a huge commotion. There were a lot of lights and people around. The sirens were what woke me up from the crash, but, I did not awake in the car. I was on the side of the road. I did not feel that I had any broken bones or injuries. I just wanted to check on Tom.

There were police and ambulance everywhere. A policeman came up to me and asked, "Madame, are you okay?" I didn't reply I was just worried about one person. Tom. I looked around for Tom. Then, I saw a sight. I thought I was hallucinating. The car was totaled. The truck was destroyed and Tom was *still* in the car.

"Tom!" I screamed. I ran towards him when two policemen stopped me. "Let go of me . . ." I shrugged.

"I am sorry, honey," one policeman said.

I looked at him at that moment. I fainted in his arms. I was rushed to the E.R. I thought I was dreaming the whole picture. Unfortunately, I was not. At the hospital my family and Tom's family were there. They were all in tears. I was in bed in a cast and I was crying. I lost my true love. Tom died in the car accident. Why? He was too young to die. He was my love. I lost the man I was going to marry. I lost my fiancé. Why would God take my love from me? Have I done something wrong to deserve this? What can I do to get him back? I want him back. It is not fair he should be here with me.

After the accident, I went home. I went to my room and was away from society. I wanted to be alone. I wanted to live on my own. I got weaker and weaker because I allowed the leukemia to get stronger and my will for life was lesser. Tom's mother planned his funeral. I went with my parents stood at his grave and said nothing to no one. Tom's funeral was one of a kind. I loved him more than she did. I know that does not make sense, but I did. I will always love him.

Nine months passed, I grew like a balloon. I was pregnant with Tom's baby. I was eager and excited to go through with it, because I knew I was going to have my baby. I didn't care what my parents or my friends said, because my true love died and I wanted to make my point heard. My baby will be born without a father and I was not too keen on bringing the child up without my true love. I still did not accept that I lost Tom.

August 3rd, 2006, Jill came over. She was unhappy with me. She told me that I should do something about my health. I disagreed. Jill got married. I did not go to the wedding. It was not a good time to flaunt happiness. I was still in mourning. Jill had already told everyone I was pregnant and that I did not need to hide myself.

"Everyone is asking for you, Anna." Jill said.

"Why don't you tell them about me, then? You are good at that."

"Anna, Tom would not want to see you like this."

"Do not dare say his name . . . ? You have no right to say his name."

"Anna, what is wrong with you? You have been so far away from people that you have forgotten that I too was Tom's friend. I invited you to come to my wedding and you did not come. Why?"

"Leave me alone, Jill. You have no idea what I am going through so stop pretending like you care okay."

A hour later, Jason arrived and came into my room. He sat with us in my room. Jill was extremely pissed at me with what I said but knew that I said it because I was sad, angry, as well as, I missed Tom. Jason, on the other hand, did not know what just happened but insisted that Jill leave us alone in my room. She was skeptic with the idea but left anyway because she did not feel she was getting anywhere with me.

"Anna, Tom is dead! Deal with it!"

I glanced at him. I was fuming with what he said. I was furious with the intention of whacking him across his face. He allowed me to do that since he knew I was distressing. Being gloomy can make you do the impossible. He was sad once when he attacked me and he knew how I was feeling.

"Anna, I know you loved him and I am sorry for what I said . . . Anna . . . live your life, he would want you too."

Jason was right. I must not feel guilty for being in love with my dead lover. I will not made feel responsible also for missing him. How can you let go of something you considered would last forever?

"Jason, I know why you are here. I want to thank you, but I would rather be on my own."

"Anna, you are pregnant. We all know you are and we know that the baby is Tom's. We are proud of you Anna that you kept yourself away from society and people but please do not do the mistake of staying here all your life. We love you, Anna . . . I mean, I love you . . ."

"Thank you, Jason."

"Anna, I love you!"

"What do you mean you love me?" I asked.

"I do! I always did and I still do."

He was approaching me. I did not know what to expect from him. I knew he wanted to do something to me but I did not know what. Then he came in for a kiss. He kissed my lips. We were kissing for a few seconds. For the seconds that we kissed, I forgot that I was sad and I missed someone because I needed to feel loved again, but then I felt water coming out of me like a fountain. I screamed.

"My water broke!"

He loves me. I thought to myself while struggling to get out. I am still in love with Tom. I will always love Tom and I will give birth to his baby. Jason helped me up out of my chair. We walked for the door. He rushed me to the hospital. He called my family and told Jill where he was.

At the hospital I was in labor. Again, a second time of my life, I experienced love and pain; love for giving birth to my baby and pain for giving birth. I was pushing and screaming and pushing and the doctor finally saw the baby; but the baby was dead. I relaxed myself in the hospital bed waiting to see my baby in my arms. Whilst I heard the most traumatizing words I thought I would never hear.

"Call it . . ." the doctor ordered.

"5:15pm, Madame;" stated the nurse.

What had happened? I did exactly what I was supposed to. I did exactly what I was told to do. I gave birth and I lost my baby . . . how could that be? I demanded to hold my baby no matter what and the doctor said no. What is God doing to me? What did I do to deserve this? Why is he causing me so much pain? Why? I demanded to see my baby and hold him in my hands. She insisted that it was very bad for me to say goodbye to someone who was not going to be with me. I insisted more than her and she agreed. The baby was living inside me for nine months I had the right to see it.

August 3rd, 2006, the birth and death of my baby boy with no name. Is God trying to tell me something? Did I do something wrong? What am I supposed to do now? Why God? Why would you do this to me? Why me? Why Tom? Why my baby? Why?

I asked the doctor to tell my parents and everyone else waiting for me outside that my baby is dead and that I decided to stay a while in the hospital until I got better. She agreed and did what I asked. She told them and my parents wanted to see me but I did not feel like seeing anyone at all.

The next day I woke up feeling healthier than ever. It was like a miracle. I did not have leukemia anymore. The doctors came in with a disbelief in their eyes and were shocked when my results came back as WOW. My leukemia was no longer part of me and I was healthy as a fully grown horse. *Music to my ears* I thought to myself. I got up and dressed and went straight to the graveyard where Tom was buried and I saw a small grave beside him.

Beautiful Baby Boy
August 3rd 2006
Birth and Death

I was happy that Tom was not alone and that our baby was with him, but also, I had to let go and that is what I decided to do. I placed my engagement ring on Tom's grave letting him know that I am ready to let go and move on. *I love you, Tom, I will always love you no matter what; but, not that both of you have left my life, it is a sign for me that I am meant to be here alive and well. I need to live my life and I will see you soon, maybe,* I thought to myself.

I went home. My parents were eagerly waiting for me. They hugged me. They told me that I should be strong and everything was going to turn out better. I told them I no longer have acute leukemia. At first they did not believe me but later, mum remembered the conversation with the doctor a year ago and she surely believed I was healthy and able to live a happy life.

Later that day, I phoned Jill to meet me at the Love Shack. I texted both Jason and Mike to meet me there as well; they did not know what to expect. I went to the Love Shack and sat at the V.I.P. Section waiting for them. While waiting for them, I felt a sudden chill down my spine. It was weird, as if I was not meant to wait for them or even talk to them face to face. Nevertheless, I did not bother with the chill.

Abruptly, I felt the chill again and it was deeper than the first chill. It got me worried so I got up this time, without avoiding the chill. I texted Jill, Jason and Mike told them I was leaving. They texted me back that they were almost there and that I should wait. I felt very rude when I got up. Then, the chill passed my spine once more time and that was my sign. I should not wait for them. I should just leave and go on my way.

That is what I did. Prior to leaving, I texted them each a different message to their phones.

Jill. You will always be my best friend and my sister. I know it is hard for you to read this from me but I cannot be here. I love you Jill and I will always think of you, but I have to go and I hope you forgive me for doing it in this way and wish me the best of luck.

Mike. Be nice to your girlfriend and try to settle down; I know you have it in you and I know it is possible for a guy like you to fall in love and have a happy life. You are part of the reality now. Make it a working and happy one since you are still around. You have a great future and life ahead of you. Do not mess it up! Mike, be active and stop your bad habits you have good things going with Sally. Marry her!

Jason. You shocked me when you told me you loved me. I never knew your feelings were still there. I am glad they are. Those feelings; you should harvest them and make them useful. Go out, fall in love all over again and let go of me! I do not love you and I do not think I will ever come back.

It is hard for me to go away but to be. Honestly, Jason, this is good for me and for you! We must make a new life for ourselves and I am doing this for me now.

I left the Love Shack. They arrived a few minutes later expecting to see me instead they did not. As they were reading their messages, Jill had tears in her eyes and she did not believe that I could do that to her. She was expecting me to tell her face-to-face but it was hard for me and that is what she did not understand. I just could not look at any of them anymore. They all reminded me of Tom. Tom was gone and I wanted to go too, and I did.

I got into a cab and left my old life. My family and friends and my two people that I thought I would live a wonderful life with; but instead I lost them both. I, Anna, am ready to go on my long lost trip that involved being away. I am ready to embark on a journey of new and undiscovered adventures that involved writing. While approaching my destination, I opened my lap top for the first time and began. I started writing my story. I always wanted to be a writer. Maybe I had to go throughout all this to see the true happiness to live and to write was what I have lived and to guide the wonderful folks out there how to go through their lives. Finally, I arrived.

*   *   *

A year past since I left home, I was constantly thinking about Tom. The images in my mind of days and hours that I spent with him were so real but yet not there. I remembered his smell and his smile. I still love him and I always will. It has been a year since I spoke to anyone in my family or any of my friends.

It is now August 2007, I am twenty-two years old; I think it is great to be lonely on your own so that you can rebut and unwind and allow the new to enter your life, whatever the new might be. A girl moved in with me the last six months. Her name is Cathy Olsen and she is a model. She is pretty cool. She is about my age and she looks exactly like Mandy Moore when she was a young blond girl. She is very friendly and loves to party.

She takes me everywhere with her. Last month she got engaged to her four year boyfriend.

I was happy yet a little jealous. I met Patrick six months ago when he was helping Cathy to move in. I partied with both of them many times. Sometimes, I went out with Patrick on our own when Cathy was at work. She was cool with that because she was the one who told us to go out together. She insisted that I meet Patrick's friends.

I remember the first day I met Patrick, I felt this tingle in me as if it was telling me that I had feelings for him. Despite the fact that he was with Cathy, every time I saw him I felt something. Every party we went to, I was looking at him; staring in a way that I wanted him to be mine. At times, he and I we out on our own, I was scared that I might do something, but I controlled myself to the extent where my feelings were locked inside me. However, regardless of the feeling, I did not do anything because Cathy is a great friend, and second, I am not that type of girl.

Patrick Thomson is a soldier. He is a well-rounded individual. He is always assigned to destinations but when he comes back he is loaded with gifts for Cathy. Sometimes he gets us both gifts. Secretly I feel he likes me like I like him but it is weird now that they are engaged. We are never told where he is assigned to. They are usually top secret missions. Cathy is madly in love with him.

It is now August 15th, 2007. It is one of the hottest days of the year. Many people advise us to stay indoors due to the galactic sun rays beamed down to earth. I believe that this is a very religious day. It is Saint Mary's birthday and everyone celebrates it by attending Church and by carnivals in her name. I am not religious at all and do not do any Church or activity involving religion, but I do believe in God.

When God gives you a hot day, I believe that we should salvage it and enjoy every moment; but contrary to my beliefs, I can be a bit of a party pooper. I felt that I just wanted to stay in today, because well, I did not feel in the mood to do anything at all. I like hanging out with Cathy and Patrick, but I hate being the third wheel which I am half the time.

Cathy and Patrick insanely planned this day for me to go out and chill with them, but not on our own, with his mate Steven. At first I declined because I did not like being set up. Then, Cathy insisted that I should expand my horizons a bit. *What is the worst that could happen* I thought?

They did it to a point that they hooked us up. Steven and Patrick are on the same force together and they practically go everywhere together. Today, both Cathy and Patrick made it a point that I met Steven and he met me. Finally, I was literally forced out of bed due to both Patrick and Cathy's insane notion to take a boat trip, on Steven's boat.

Since I was forced on this God forsaken trip, I decided to look my best. Cathy has seen Steven many times and she bragged to me about how buff he is whenever we were alone. I have never seen him so I pictured the images in my mind when she used to talk about him. I was ready in my room waiting for the time to pass when the doorbell rang. I thought Cathy was home, but it seems both Patrick and Cathy were out so I went to open the door. To my disclosure, Steven was standing outside. He was told by Patrick to come to the house and wait for them.

I allowed him in. He was glaring at me. He was staring as if we have met before in another life or so I thought. Steven is pretty cute, though. He has that rugged type of handsome look. I just could not stop looking at him. While gazing in each other's eyes, we both sat at the same time on a couch beside each other.

"Anna, it is really nice to meet you." Steven stated while trying to break the ice which was plated upon our gazes. "Anna, you are hot. I told Patrick I could take you out but he insisted that we double for this boat trip that I am not so fond of. Are you?"

"To be honest, no, I am not at all and I would rather just sit in for the day." I answered.

"It is settled then. We go out and leave the two love birds on their own. Sounds cool?"

I could not stop looking at him. His eyes, his mouth, his lips . . . Oh my God, what sweet lips he has. I really want to just grab him and kiss him but before I could, in come the love birds, hand in hand.

"Are we ready for the boat ride mates?" Patrick asked while winking his eye at me then at Steven.

"I do not feel well." I stated hoping I would be allowed to be lazy and yet, no was the answer I had to go with them.

"Anna, you are not getting out of this at all!" Insisted Patrick.

I took Cathy aside and asked her if we could do the boat ride another time. She disagreed.

"Patrick and Steven asked their colonel if they could take two days off now so they could hang out with us." She stated in a low but very firm voice.

She begged me to go because she did not want to go on her own with Patrick and Steven.

"Okay Mr. Pirate; let us be on our way out to sea!" I exclaimed.

We arrived at the docks. We got into the boat. It was a cozy small boat which is only used for cruises basically. Cathy and I went into the cabin to change into our bikinis so we could sunbathe on the boat while Patrick and Steven were chatting about us. Steven was fascinated with me that he wanted to get to know more of me.

"Cathy, can I talk to Anna for a moment please?" Steven asked while approaching the sun deck of the boat.

He stood beside us and suddenly took his shirt off. His six-pack was glowing in the sunlight which gave me complete Goosebumps all over my body. My body began tingling quickly while he was turning to sit beside me. After he sat down, he was stretching his arms so that he could try to hug me. I assumed.

"Anna." He said with a smile on his face.

"Yes," I replied while still feeling the Goosebumps down my body.

"You make me, want to, do, this," he moved in for the kiss but I got up quickly and ran inside the cabin.

Why did I do that? He will think I am a weirdo or a freak. I thought to myself. Cathy ran in.

"Are you kidding me?" Cathy asked.

"I do not know what happened."

"You do not know?"

"No. I don't."

"I will tell you what happened . . . You are very weird and silly."

After she said that to me with full force she went out on the deck and sat with Steven. I was embarrassed with my action but I was not ready, well I know I was ready, but I felt it was so wrong to kiss someone without getting to know them a little bit. I felt ashamed to go outside. Patrick walked in to comfort me.

"I am not weird." I said while tears where rolling down my face.

He approached me and hugged me then he said, "No, you are not. I am sure Cathy did not mean what she said."

"Patrick. I am just scared. I, well, I . . ." I could not finish my statement; I hugged Patrick. Despite him coming round we never shook hands or anything. It was always a wave or a gesture.

He pulled me off him. Surprisingly, everything changed between the two of us. Our feelings for one another were too confusing to make out and as a replacement for my unexpected hug to him, he looked at me like he has never looked at me before; and then he moved in for the kiss.

Out of the blue, I did not stop him; I allowed him to kiss me and I kissed him back. We were kissing for about forty-five seconds. It drove me wild while kissing him. He was getting excited too but we both realized what we were doing, while being on board with one person we both know and love very much; we know and respect and even find as family, we stopped abruptly and re-evaluated our situation.

"What have I done?" He asked.

"What just happened? Why did it happen? I did not mean for this to happen. What have I done?" I corrected.

"No, you were telling me what you felt and you needed a shoulder but I never touched you, not even your hand. It is weird because I feel I want you more now than ever before."

"Excuse me?"

"Anna, I am sorry. I think I am in love with you."

"No, you cannot be in love with me. You are engaged to Cathy, remember?" I stopped him from creating a mistake.

"What do I do now?" he asked.

"Pretend this never happened; it never did." I informed him it was a bad idea to do it here and now; plus, she is my roommate and Steven is his friend.

"Are you sure? Is it what you want?"

"I do not know what I want and neither do you, but what I do know that Cathy loves you very much and it will be hard for us to be in this situation unless one of us comes clean."

He walked out onto the deck. I sat there wondering. What happened? I thought to myself. I mean seriously, that is what I have now become. Now, stealing my friend's fiancé? Come on, I cannot be this now. It is not good for me. I cannot handle this now. This is way too bad to say the least. This is impossible to forget but must never be said out in public.

I just cannot explain what action I have taken by allowing myself to kiss him, but it was like I wanted it for some time, and I actually went for it; but it is not okay to do something like this. I know she will not forgive me. She would call me a relationship-wrecker and many other words I cannot think of now; Patrick has a gorgeous gaze and when we locked eyes, I could not break free.

I wanted to strip his clothes off and make love to him. However, that was not likely to happen now, or ever. What have I done? Who have I become? Actually, the true question here is, what have I become?

While I was rambling to myself, Cathy came inside and sat beside me. She was sad but I had no idea why. Then Patrick and Steven came inside. Steven looked at me and then at Cathy and then back at me. No one was saying anything. They were like stunned school kids on their first trip to la-la land.

"What is going on? Why are you silent?" I asked.

"Cathy and Steven were making out and instead of me getting pissed at them, Cathy got mad at me because I did not react." Patrick replied.

"Wait? What?" I exclaimed.

"Anna, I am sorry, I know you were supposed to be with Steven but he kind of flirted with me and I went for it. My real surprise though is my so-called fiancé who did not over react." Cathy stated, "it is like he has done something too, and he does not want to look like the bad guy."

"Steven is my friend and now you are my ex-fiancé." Patrick continued.

She got annoyed with his remark and then he whispered in her ear, "if you want me to react, here," he approached me and French-kissed me.

The other out of the blue moment we felt again. It, though, did not feel out of the blue and made me feel more excited. I allowed him to kiss me and I enjoyed it and so did he; however the other party, not so much.

"Excuse me?" I asked, pretending to feel out of order from the ordeal of kissing *my friend's fiancé*.

"I am sorry. There. Now, we are fair." He looked me in my eye and gave the look as if it was the first time and I honestly went along with it.

Patrick walked out and sat on the deck on his own. Then, Cathy followed him and started to ask for forgiveness. I was sure he was going to tell her that he doesn't love her anymore but I was not sure if I could live in the same apartment as her while he would be telling her who he has feelings for.

Steven approached me and sat beside me, "so, we both kissed others and not each other."

After stating the obvious, he moved in for his turn to kiss me. We spend a long fifty seconds on this very passionate kiss. I enjoyed it. The kiss was too intense that I was feeling things I should not have but I was feeling. I really have feelings for Patrick but that did not seem that it was going to happen anytime soon. For some pathetic reason, I gave in to Steven's kiss.

"Anna, marry me?" He asked me.

"What do you mean marry you?" I gasped.

That was the first moment, when I just saw that I was kissing Tom that I blurted out, "I am yours Steven, yes, I will marry you." I was shocked with my own behavior that Steven locked the cabin door. Patrick turned in a quick frenzy and started banging on the door. He was so mad that he might have missed his opportunity with me. Well, come on, I have been around for a while and you are the fiancé of my roommate Cathy, I cannot be with you.

Steven took off all his clothes and stood there in complete full orgasmic throttle that allowed me to feel pleasure without being touched. *Tom, forgive me, I love you, I will always love you and you will always be my first, but I have been wanting this since well, since I lost you.* I thought to myself while stripping off my sexy, green bikini.

He approached me and began man-handling massaging my breasts while hearing me moan in excitement. It was so good that I felt like just pulling him on top of me. *I think I love you, Steven.* I spoke to myself while having sex. He was grinding up against me and for the first time it wasn't the sweet love making, it was the vulgar sex that I have not experienced but it hurt so much more than the first time I lost my virginity. I was about to make him stop but he just about finished and quickly pulled out from inside me so his sperm would not infect my eggs *or so how he stated while he finished sex with me.*

Astoundingly, he got up, got dressed and told me to do the same and went out on the deck. I was sitting there mesmerized by what happened wondering why he would just get up and leave me alone in the cabin. I got dressed and went outside. I sat beside him. He was acting absurd around me as if nothing happened and as if he did not say what he said in the cabin.

"Steven, can I talk to you for a minute please?" I asked him politely.

We went into the cabin and I sat on the chair while he was standing like a stud. He thought I wanted to have sex with him another time so he pulled me towards him. He began kissing me vulgarly. I struggled to break free because that is not what I wanted. He clutched his arms around me and began man-handling my breasts again. I then broke one of my hands free and pushed him off me.

"What are you doing? Why are you acting like this?"

"What do you want from me?" He asked.

"Steven, you just asked me to marry you; what is going on?"

He grabbed me again and went in for another kiss. At first I did not know what he was trying to do. Then he whispered in my ear, "let's have sex again and I will marry you, I promise."

"No! Marry me and maybe I'll think about it."

"No way! Have sex with me and maybe I will marry you."

"Maybe? You told me that you would before."

"And you believed me, I am a guy and I would say anything to sleep with a girl and someone as pretty as yourself."

"You used me?" I began tearing up.

"Anna, it is not like you are a virgin to worry about being used. It was just sex and I thought you had fun; plus how in the hell will I marry you if I know nothing about you. Imagine, we just met and you slept with me, how can I marry someone who would do something like that?"

I was tearing and the tears could not stay in my eyes. They just blurted out. I got up, slapped him on his face; I never knew I was sex-ing a prick. I felt so ashamed and disgusted that I left the cabin and ran straight for the deck and abruptly jumped overboard. He was furious with the slap but did not expect me to react the way I did.

Now, this part of the conversation, made me feel so bad that I wanted to just drown. I am sure many of you girls have been through it and it is so painful. It hurts like fire. It hurts like knives pulsating into my heart. It hurts so much that I feel I am going to just drown myself.

After I jumped, Steven came out onto the deck, "where is she?"

"What happened?" Cathy asked in disappointment.

"We had a fight and she slapped me."

"What did you say to her, Steven?" Patrick asked.

"Nothing, she just got all freaked out because we just slept together and that she wanted us to become an item and I do not do relationships."

"You slept together?" Cathy asked in amazement. Patrick was mad because he wanted to do that.

While arguing, I still have not approached the surface of the water. Patrick felt weary about the situation that he jumped in after me. He swam deep down and still could not find me. He went up again for air.

"Did you find her?" Cathy asked.

"No." Patrick stated.

He went back down again trying his best to find me. While he was trying to save me, I found myself looking closer and closer to a white light. Well, I should have since I wanted to let go of my life and the mistake I have done and the words I heard.

As an alternative, I saw something I was not meant to see. I saw flashes of my family and how sad they were for me. It seems that mum was the saddest of all because she thought so as to growing old I would be right by her. I saw dad sitting at his desk in his study writing away at his journals and waiting for me to go home.

Then, another flash past; it was a flash of me and Jill. She is my best friend but I never in a million years felt that I would be away from her and yet I am. My flash of her is about her being pregnant and happy in her marriage but missing me terribly.

Subsequently, I saw a flash of both Jason and Mike who became closer after I left them to be. I see them working together owning their own night club; being the players that they were always. Though, I see in Jason's wallet a picture of me and him when we were dating.

Suddenly, I see the one person I never in a century thought I would see. Tom. He came to me and hugged me and told me, "Anna, it is not your time and that you still have your life ahead of you."

"Tom, I love you and I miss you terribly."

"Anna, baby, you cannot come with me."

"Why not, I need to be with you. My life is nothing without you. Baby, I cannot live like this. You are always in my mind and I cannot do this anymore."

"Yes you can Anna. Let go of me like you did a while ago and you should let go so you will be saved by your new companion that will take my place. Baby, trust me when I say this, I will always love you and I know you will always love me but this is the truth of the matter and I must go and you must let me go!"

"I cannot!"

"Goodbye Anna!"

"Tom, no, please, do not leave me! Please! Tom!"

I wanted to stay with him so bad, I was drifting further and further away into the deep end of the sea. All of a sudden, Patrick found me, grabbed my arm, pulled me out of the water and onto the deck; he gave me mouth-to-mouth and saved my life. A few seconds more and I would have died. He put me in the cabin and I was lying down asleep while Patrick drove the boat back to the harbor. I was sound asleep and felt nothing from the rest of the trip. Patrick took me to the hospital.

Cathy went home to pack her things because she felt she was out of line. She moved out of the apartment and went to live with her sister. She send Patrick a text message saying:

Patrick, I love you. I know that we would have been great together. However, ever since Anna came along, you and I have not been the item we were meant to be. We were just an image there for show. It is sad because I know you love me too. I think we need time apart and I will miss you terribly. Tell Anna I am sorry for everything and I did not mean to say what I did. I am leaving the ring in her apartment. Thank you for a few wonderful years together. I will never forget you, but I will let go of you. Take care. Love always Cathy.

The odd part is that she did not come to see me in the hospital. She did not even call me. She just disappeared. I was in the hospital for a week. Within that week, Patrick was with me from morning to night. Patrick never spoke to Steven again. He, on the other hand, surprised me and called my parents. At first they did not like what they heard then, they figured they should come down and see me. Also, my mother called Jill, Jason and Mike to come and see me, if they wanted to.

My parents insisted I go back home. At first, I did not want to leave but then, I agreed and told them that I would want to take things slow no matter how long it would take and they agreed. Jill, Mike and Jason were over the moon about my return that they decided to celebrate. Patrick on the other hand, was not too enthusiastic about the whole move but faked his happiness for me.

Patrick was the type that would never give up. He made it seem too easy but in reality it was not. He entered my room in the hospital and gave me some advice I did not know why he even did. I mean he called my parents and now he is telling me not to leave? I was too confused and taken by surprise. I know where he is coming from, but why would I not go back. Then, Tom appeared in my mind. There was something Tom said to me to make me want to change my mind.

I was asked to be alone for a while to think. *I did this. I left to start over. I decided on my own to make that stupid move with Steven. I decided on my own to drown myself. I did it all by myself. I did it; me; only me. Why do I feel that I have failed? Only if I go back home I have failed.* Then, I thought to myself, *why would I fail if I go back? Why would I be a failure? I would not be one if I go back and face my demons.*

I sat there thinking to myself for the past two hours wondering what was going to be my answer to everyone. Tom, will always be in my heart, but I let go of him the moment I met Patrick. Ever since I met Patrick things in me changed, feelings that I thought I would never feel again, I feel them with him and it is strange because my love for Tom is and will always be there but Patrick made me feel better about myself and made me want to live. Before I gave birth though, Jason told me he still loved me. My feelings for Jason are still there but I do not know really what they are.

The feelings for Jason are more complicated. There was an incident that happened a while ago, when I was still Tom's girlfriend, Jason approached me in a vulgar way. What makes me so sure that his vulgar way will not happen again? I do not know him very well to say yes, he is the man for me. I may go off with him and feel *wait a minute, I am in the wrong relationship* or even maybe, he might be the man for me and his vulgar ways are over because he said he loves me. I know I have feelings for both of these boys but which one is stronger I do not know. I asked to speak with Jason on our own.

Jason came in and sat on my bed. He was stroking my hand as if we were an item once again. I was staring at him trying to understand what feelings I have for him. What makes Jason special? What makes me smile when I see him? What makes me tingle when I think of him?

"I am glad you are coming home." Jason said while 'breaking the ice'.

"I have not decided yet. I am still thinking about it."

"Why not? What is stopping you?"

"Jason, remember the night I gave birth, you said something to me."

"Oh, yeah, that night. Well, I . . ."

"What Jason? What did you mean by those words?"

"I love you and I still do till now."

"Do you?"

"Yes . . . I do. I always will."

"Jason. I loved you once and you lost me. What makes you sure that it will work again?"

"Anna, the love I feel for you is just like that night we were going to make love."

"Was it real?"

"Yes, and it still is real."

"Are you sure Jason?"

"Yes!"

"Jason, I am not a toy you can bounce around whenever you feel like it. Though, I do not think you are sure."

"Anna, please, listen to me when I say this, my only pleasure is to see you happy where ever it may be. If this happiness is with me I would appreciate it even more. If it is again, not with me, then I will gladly let you go. However, I know how much you love me. I do know that."

"My love for you is danced out by this whole mix up. Why tell me your feelings now? Where were you when I disappeared for a year and wanted time off? Did you get in contact with me? Did you fight for me? No!! How can I believe what you are saying now?"

"Anna, you are not a toy and I know that very well and you know I know that. That point is cleared out. The day that I received that text message from you was the day I felt I lost you. I did not give up. I prayed everyday to get you to come back."

"You prayed? Jason, please I am not nine years old for me to believe you prayed."

"I did pray. Believe what you want. I did nothing but try to fix myself up and get myself set so the day that I will see you again I will try my best to offer you the life you always dreamed to have; a life with me, a happy life."

"Jason, I think I believe you."

He actually thought I was serious and it was sad because I was trying to understand my feelings that are divided amongst two great, good looking guys. He went down on one knee and proposed to me. At that moment, I wish it had not happened, because Patrick walked in. Patrick was shocked that he just wanted to flee. In turn, he did not because the motion that was in his legs was officially glued to the ground.

"Will you marry me, Anna?"

Jason was so sure of what I was going to say. He knew that I loved him in some way or form but did not know which way. I did not know what to say. I just sat there. Then, he got up and asked me again and I still didn't say anything. Patrick, being so sure he was in the wrong place answered the question for me.

"Jason, my good man, of course she will marry you." Patrick stated.

He came towards Jason and me, hugged him and said congratulations to both of us and left. I did not answer but my silence meant something to Patrick. I got up out of bed and ran towards Patrick. I told Jason I was going to be back so he sat on my hospital bed to wait for me.

"Why did you say that?" I grabbed Patrick's arm and pulled him towards me.

"I saw how excited you were and I am sure your answer would have been yes, because you saw me, you went silent." Patrick said.

"No, you jerk, I would have said no."

I honestly, was not expecting Jason to follow me out and he did. He heard what I said and I was kind of in the dilemma of the oh my God phrase.

"Is that what you would have said, Anna?" Jason asked.

I turned around as slow as possible for neither of the boys to flee. I grabbed them both and tried to make myself as clear as possible but I did not get anywhere with either of them; or so I thought. I looked at Jason with an open heart.

"Jason, you are my best friend and when you kissed me the day I gave birth to my baby boy, everything changed between us. I knew it did and I am glad it did. When you did what you did, I sort of panicked. I know that kiss was because of guilt rather than love or maybe it was love, but Jason, you and I were in love a long time ago. My feelings for you, Jason, are not love. I realized that when the one I love walked out of the door."

I turned round and paid full attention to Patrick. I looked him in his eyes and said what I never in my whole years would have said if he did not kiss me on the boat and I was glad he did because I was dying to do that ever since I met him. I know that is wrong but when your heart locks on an individual, you have nothing to do then wait for the right moment to explode your feelings for that person.

"Patrick, the day you walked in my apartment and you were presented to me as Cathy's fiancé, I was so shocked because my heart locked onto you. I love you. I never hoped for it to happen but it did and when we kissed on the boat, I felt my whole body tingle. I did not expect myself to fall in love again, but I did and I am glad because I want to be with you and only you."

"Anna, I cannot see myself without you. I am in love with you. I have been building a life for me and you so that one day you will come back to me." Jason exclaimed.

"Jason, this is not a movie and no I will not go back to the person I used to love, I loved you once but not any more though I know truly in my heart we would have been great together. The day you attacked me everything changed and the day you kissed me made me realize I was wronging myself if I were to go back and I do not want to go back. I want to move forward and be loved anew and honestly that is what happened and I did love anew. I know Jason, I know you love me. It is hard to move on but you have to. Jason, you are an amazing guy, but you are not my guy."

"Anna, I love you; but if you truly feel that Patrick will make you happy then I will let go of you as you want me to. I wish you the best of luck, both of you!" Jason said with all his heart, a heart I thought I would never experience and to the saddest part of my thought it happened later than it should have.

"You love me?" Patrick asked in confusion.

"Yes, jerk, I love you." I stated.

"I love you, too." He replied with delight.

Patrick grabbed me and pulled me towards his lips. We kissed. While kissing, Jason walked away and explained to my parents, Jill and Mike that I will not be coming home with them. My life is here with Patrick. Jason, then, left. Patrick and I went to my family and friends and told them basically what Jason said.

Jill and Mike left also without saying goodbye. I realized that I did not need my friends to be happy or I did not need to be with them in the same town to be happy; I found my contentment elsewhere and honestly, neither of my alleged friends liked my decision. Well, *tough cookie*, I am going to be where I want to.

My parents were the happiest ever that I decided to be strong and live a new journey that was started and should continue in order to surpass the past that I promised to let go of from the beginning. Patrick took me home and moved in with me. My life has never been better than it is today. I still love my parents but now, it is my time to make my adventures and dreams come true.